Questions, Questions

Copyright © 2011 by NordSüd Verlag AG, CH-8005 Zürich, Switzerland.
First published in Switzerland under the title *Was macht die Farben bunt?*
English text copyright © 2011 by North-South Books Inc., New York 10001.
Translated by NordSüd Verlag. English adaptation by Marcus Pfister and Susan Pearson.
All rights reserved.
No part of this book may be reproduced or utilized in any form or by any means,
electronic or mechanical, including photo-copying, recording, or any information storage
and retrieval system, without permission in writing from the publisher.

First published in the United States, Great Britain, Canada, Australia, and New Zealand
in 2011 by North-South Books Inc., an imprint of NordSüd Verlag AG, CH-8005 Zürich, Switzerland.
Distributed in the United States by North-South Books Inc., New York 10001.

Library of Congress Cataloging-in-Publication Data is available.
Printed in China by Leo Paper Products Ltd., Heshan, Guangdong, November 2010.
ISBN: 978-0-7358-4000-3 (trade edition)
1 3 5 7 9 • 10 8 6 4 2

www.northsouth.com
Meet Marcus Pfister at www.marcuspfister.ch.

FSC
www.fsc.org
MIX
Paper from
responsible sources
FSC® C020056

Questions, Questions

Marcus Pfister

NorthSouth
New York / London

How do seeds know how to grow,
to reach up from the earth below?

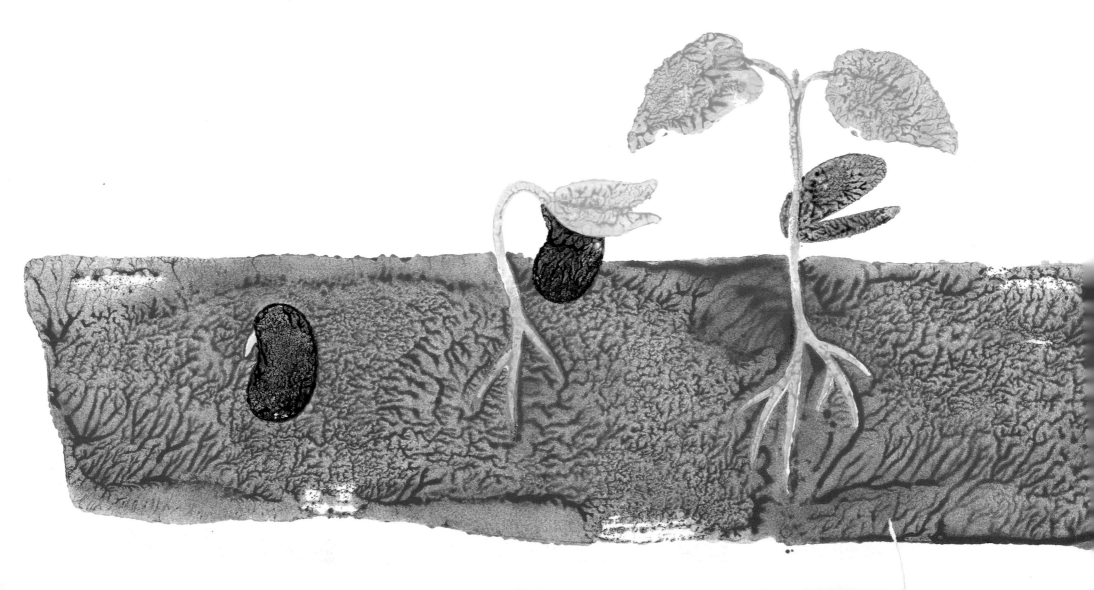

Who paints the colors on the flowers
that lift their heads to sun and showers?

What turns the rain on in the sky
and brings the sun to make things dry?

How do birds learn how to sing?

What brings summer after spring?

What turns the leaves from green to brown

and sends them floating gently down?

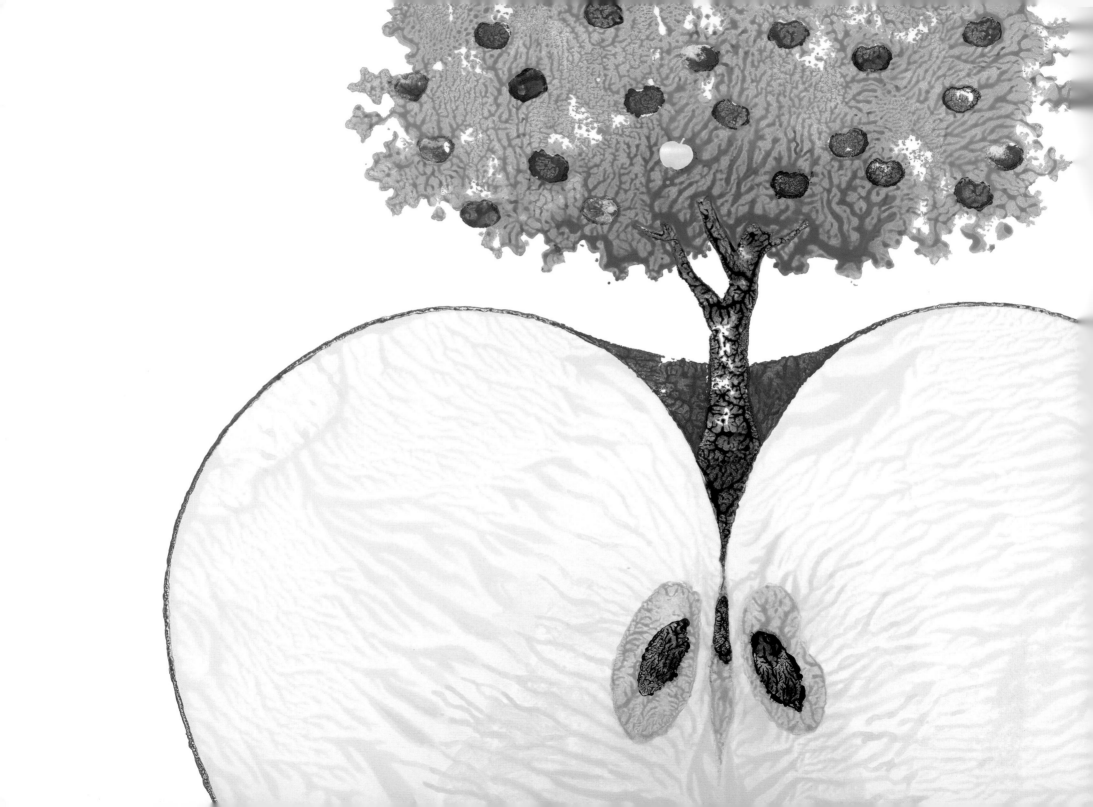

Do apple seeds dream happily
of growing up to be a tree?

How many shells are on the shore?

Millions? Billions? Even more?

How many little fish might see
the stone I throw into the sea?

Who teaches butterflies to fly,

splashing their colors through the sky?

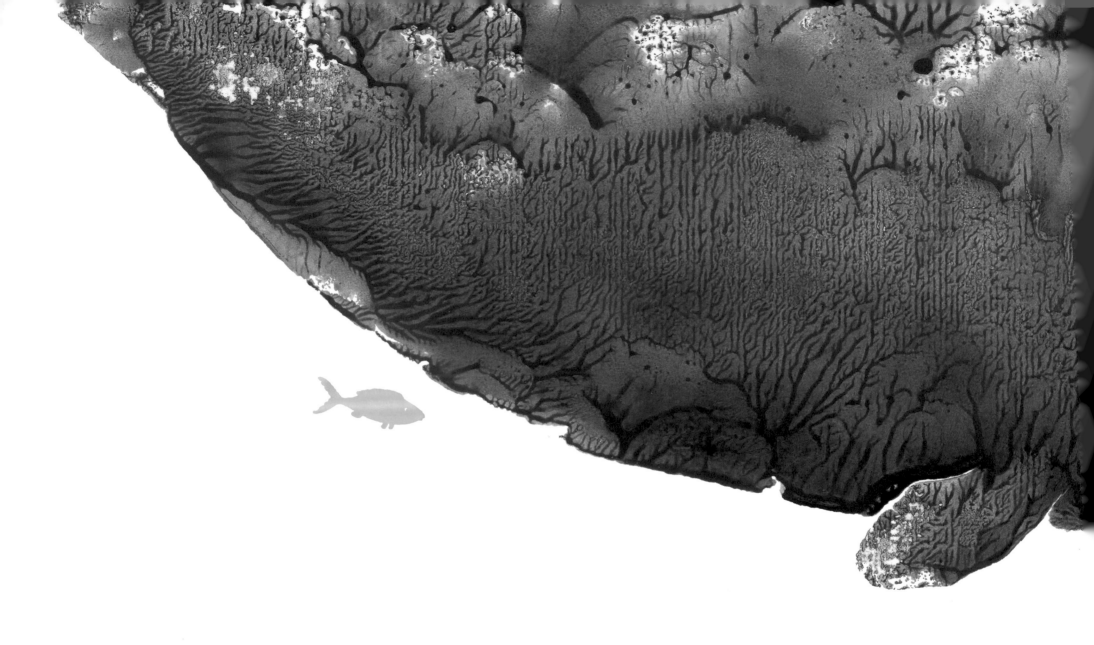

Does a whale make up a song

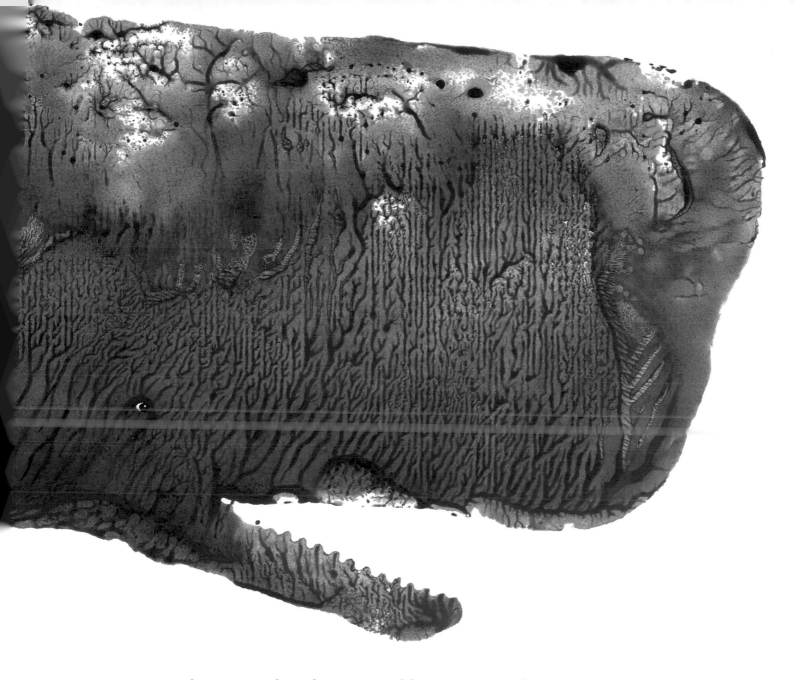

so other whales will sing along?

When geese fly south, how do they know
it's time to leave and where to go?

What makes fire burn red and gold

and makes it much too hot to hold?

Did dinosaurs eat all day long
to make them grow so big and strong?

Wind and rain, sun and snow—
there's so much that I want to know.

Birds and flowers, sea and air—
questions, questions everywhere!

ON HIS LAST ITALIAN HOLIDAY, Marcus Pfister heard an old Lucio Dalla song, "Cosa sarà," which became the inspiration for this book. "It's my first book based on a poem," he says, "and I felt it needed very simple, almost abstract illustrations, so I started to experiment with a new technique.

"First I transferred my drawing to thick cardboard. Then I cut out each piece of the drawing. I put acrylic paint on these pieces, then stamped them onto aquarelle paper, creating each illustration piece by piece.

"This technique gets quite fast and interesting results, and it's simple to do if your pieces aren't too complicated. I hope you'll try it!"